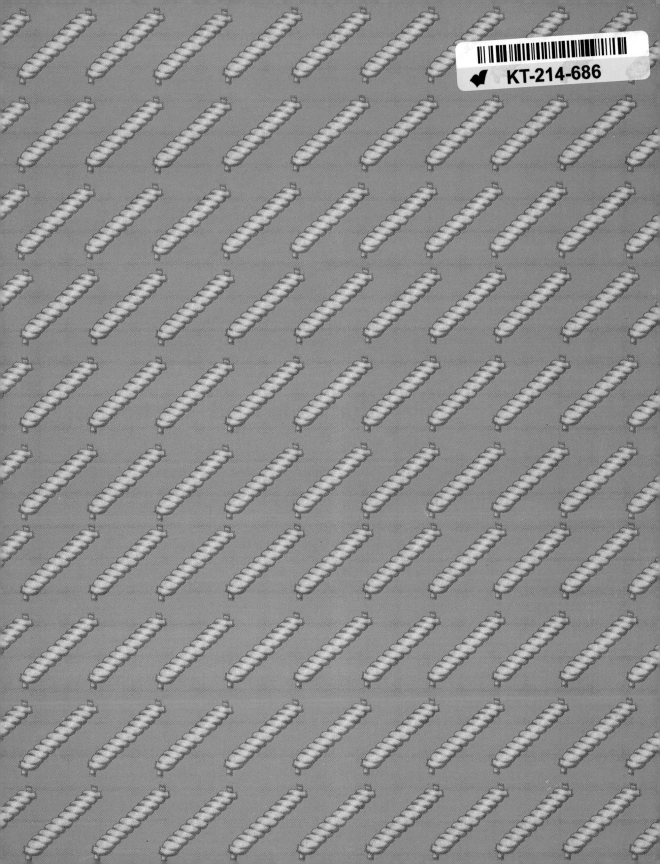

Published by
Armadillo Books
an imprint of
Bookmart Limited
Registered Number 2372865
Trading as Bookmart Limited
Desford Road
Enderby
Leicester LE9 5AD

ISBN 1-84322-004-0

Produced for
Bookmart Limited by
Nicola Baxter
PO Box 215,
Framingham Earl
Norwich NR14 7UR

Designer: Amanda Hawkes
Production designer: Amy Barton

Printed in China

Starting to read – no trouble!

This story of trouble on the ice helps to make sharing books at home successful and enjoyable. The book can be used in several ways to help beginning readers gain confidence.

You could start by reading the illustrated words at the edge of each lefthand page with your child. Have fun trying to spot the same words in the story itself.

All the words on the righthand pages have already been met on the facing page. Help your child to read these by pointing out words and groups of words already met.

Finally, all the illustrated words can be found at the end of the book. Enjoy checking all the words you can both read!

Trouble
on
The Ice

Written by Nicola Baxter · Illustrated by Geoff Ball

ARMADILLO

Rosa

Tom

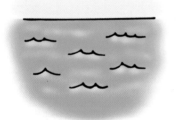
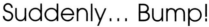

sea

ship

Rosa and Tom look out across the sea. They are on a big ship.

"When will we get there?" asks Tom.

"Soon," shouts Rosa. "Look!"

Far away, they can see a white land.

Suddenly… Bump!

"Look out!" Tom shouts.

iceberg

water

damage

anchor

The ship has hit an iceberg! Most of the iceberg is under the water.

Luckily, there is not much damage.

At last the ship's anchor is dropped.

"We're here!" cries Rosa. "No more bumps!"

Suddenly… Bump!

"Look out!" Tom cries. "Water!"

whale

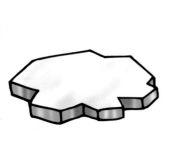

ice

boots

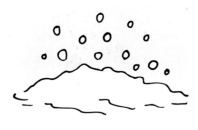

snow

Wooosh! A whale has bumped into the ship! Everyone is wet.

At last, Rosa and Tom land on the ice. They have warm, dry clothes and boots on now.

"I've never seen so much snow!" says Tom.

"No more getting wet!" says Rosa.

Suddenly… Splash!

"Look out!" Tom cries. "The ice!"

hole

rope

anorak

trousers

There is a hole in the ice! Someone has been fishing.

"I'm sliding under the ice!" cries Rosa.

"Catch hold of this rope, Rosa!" shouts Tom.

He pulls Rosa to safety.

"I'm glad my anorak and trousers are waterproof," says Rosa. "Now we must hurry."

"No more bumps and no more splashes," says Tom.

Suddenly… Wheeee!

"Look out!" Tom cries. "I'm sliding!"

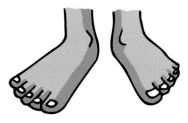

feet

bear

Rosa and Tom land in a heap.
Rosa gets to her feet.

"Come on, Tom!" she cries,
marching ahead.

hood

Something moves. It is white
like the snow. It is a bear!

Tom tries to call out.

"What?" Rosa cannot hear
with her hood up.

arms

Tom dances up and down.
He waves his arms.

So does the bear!

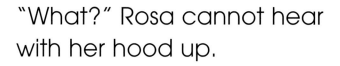

"Look out!" shouts Tom. "A bear!"

sky

rainbow

camera

hat

"He won't hurt us!" says Rosa. "Look, he's dancing!"

"Never mind that bear," says Tom. "Look at the sky!"

The sky turns all the colours of the rainbow.

"Hey! Where's my camera?" asks Tom. He even looks in his hat!

"Hey! Where's that bear?" asks Rosa.

footprints

captain

snack

photos

"Follow that bear!" shouts Rosa. But the bear's footprints are soon lost in the snow.

Rosa and Tom go back to the ship.

"Tell me about your adventures," says the captain, as they tuck into a snack. "Did you take some photos?"

"No," says Tom. "There are no photos at all."

But he is wrong.

The bear did take some photos!

Picture dictionary

Now you can read these words!

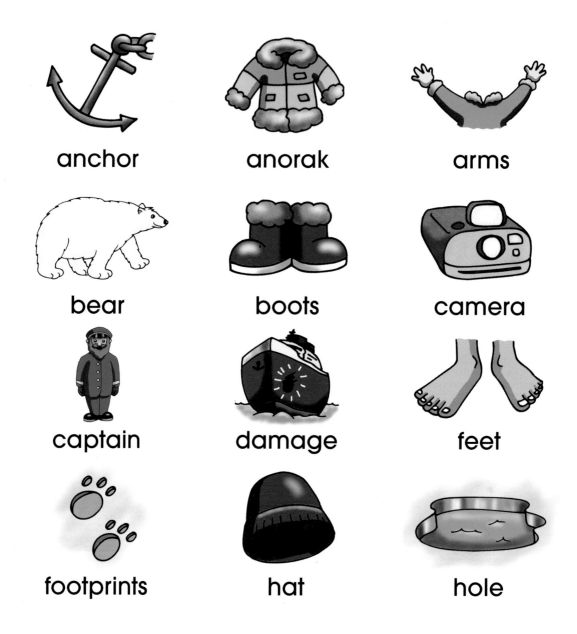

anchor

anorak

arms

bear

boots

camera

captain

damage

feet

footprints

hat

hole

 hood

 iceberg

 photos

 rainbow

 rope

 Rosa

 sea

 ship

 sky

 snack

 snow

 Tom

 trousers

 water

 whale

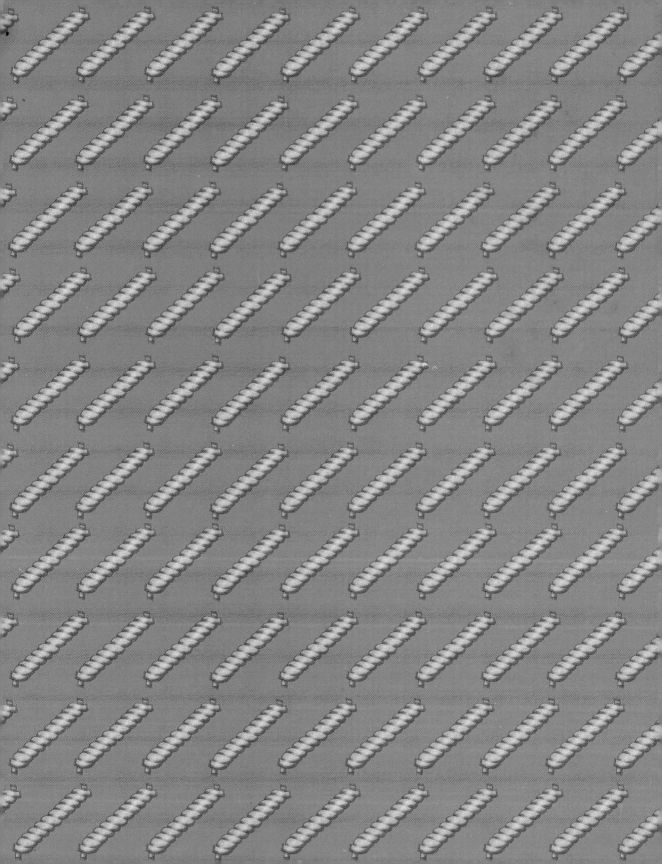